JUST A
SNOWY VACATION

BY GINA AND MERCER MAYER

*To Len,
in loving memory*

A Random House PICTUREBACK® Book

Random House New York

Just a Snowy Vacation book, characters, text, and images copyright © 2001, 2019 Gina and Mercer Mayer
Little Critter, Mercer Mayer's Little Critter, and Mercer Mayer's Little Critter Logo are registered trademarks
and Little Critter Classics and Logo is a trademark of Orchard House Licensing Company. All rights reserved.
Published in the United States by Random House Children's Books, a division of Penguin Random House LLC,
1745 Broadway, New York, NY 10019, and in Canada by Penguin Random House Canada Limited, Toronto.
Originally published in slightly different form by Golden Books, an imprint of Random House Children's Books, New York, in 2001.
Pictureback, Random House, and the Random House colophon are registered trademarks of Penguin Random House LLC.

Ornament design on front cover used under license from Shutterstock.com

Visit us on the Web! • rhcbooks.com • littlecritter.com

Educators and librarians, for a variety of teaching tools, visit us at RHTeachersLibrarians.com

ISBN 978-1-9848-3077-7 (trade) — ISBN 978-1-9848-3078-4 (ebook)

MANUFACTURED IN CHINA

10 9 8 7 6 5 4 3 2 1

Random House Children's Books supports the First Amendment and celebrates the right to read

My whole family went on vacation.
Except the baby. He stayed at Grandma's.

We drove up the mountains. There was a lot of snow up there. But we were warm because we were in the car.

We went to Critter Mountain Ski
Resort. We walked up to the front desk,
and they gave us a room.

The bellhop drove us to our room in a funny little wagon.
A bellhop is a critter that carries your stuff around so you
don't get tired.

The first night, Mom and Dad rested while
my little sister and I watched TV and played.

We woke up bright and early to hit the slopes. We had breakfast in the big dining room. It was full of critters from everywhere.

After breakfast we went to the ski rental booth to get our skis.

Dad left Mom and us at the bunny slope, and he went off to "tame the mountain." That's what he said.

I did great on the bunny slope,
but my little sister needed help.

I could stop.

I could turn.

I could jump.

I could
even do
tricks.

We saw a rescue team going up
the mountain. That was neat.

Later they brought down someone who had wiped out on the slopes. It was Dad. Poor Dad. He looked kind of upset.

They had a doctor right there. I guess
this kind of thing happens a lot.

The doctor sure bandaged Dad's
ankle up real good.

Dad had to rest. We put him in bed and made
him comfy before we went back out to have fun.

Mom, Little Sister, and I took a ride on the ski lift. My little sister was scared, but I wasn't.

After that we went ice-skating. Dad came out to watch. I called, "Hey, Dad, neat crutches."

He just waved.

In the morning, we packed up. My little sister and I helped a lot.

The bellhop loaded up our car.
He even let Dad keep the crutches.
Mom had to drive all the way home.

Wasn't that fun, Dad?